The Abduction of Queen Guinevere

by

BARAK A. BASSMAN

TELEMACHUS PRESS

This book is a work of fiction. Names, characters, places and incidents are either the product of the author's imagination or are used fictitiously. Any resemblance to actual persons, living or dead, or to actual events or locales is entirely coincidental.

THE ABDUCTION OF QUEEN GUINEVERE
Copyright © 2022 Barak A. Bassman. All rights reserved, including the right to reproduce this book, or portions thereof, in any form. No part of this text may be reproduced, transmitted, downloaded, decompiled, reverse engineered, or stored in or introduced into any information storage and retrieval system, in any form or by any means, whether electronic or mechanical without the express written permission of the author. The scanning, uploading, and distribution of this book via the Internet or via any other means without the permission of the author and publisher is illegal and punishable by law. Please purchase only authorized electronic editions and do not participate in or encourage electronic piracy of copyrighted materials.

The publisher does not have any control over and does not assume any responsibility for author or third-party websites or their content.

Cover design by Telemachus Press, LLC

Cover art:
Copyright © iStock/1204393214/_U_09

Publishing Services by Telemachus Press, LLC
7652 Sawmill Road
Suite 304
Dublin, Ohio 43016
http://www.telemachuspress.com

ISBN: 978-1-956867-17-6 (eBook)
ISBN: 978-1-956867-19-0 (Paperback)

Library of Congress Control Number: 2022900652

Version 2022.01.16

Table of Contents

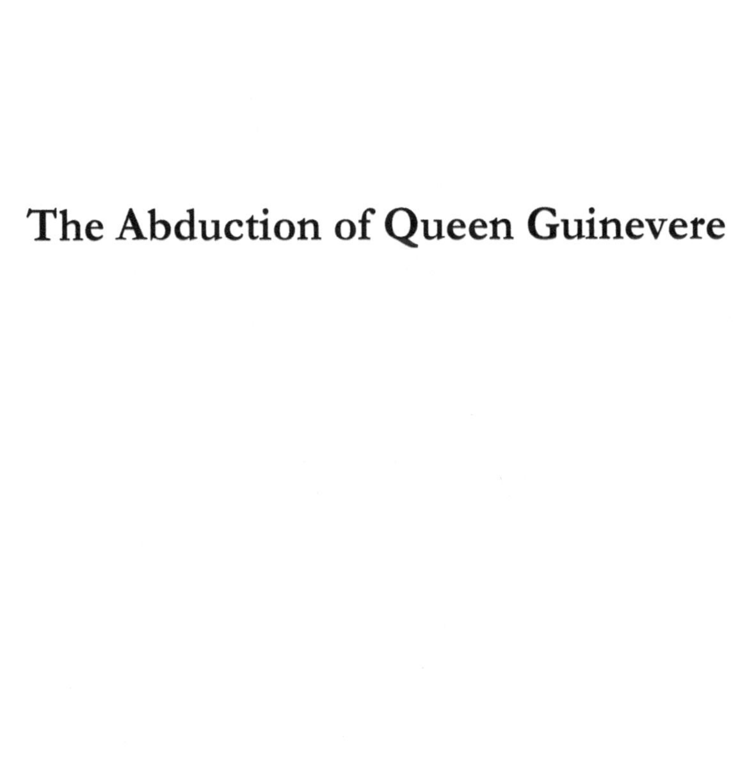

The Abduction of Queen Guinevere

I. The Challenge

IT HAD BEEN a splendid day at Camelot—sunny and warm, the air not too heavy, and he had felled a large boar during the morning hunt. Now reclining on a couch in his great hall, King Arthur was discussing with several knights his plans for hosting a new tournament in the coming months.

But then, as twilight was gently descending through the tall windows, a knight in silver armor burst into the hall, tore off his helmet, pointed his forefinger at the King, and said: Arthur, son of Uther Pendragon, King of Logres, you have stolen my wife and taken her into your bed. I demand you return her to me now, without any delay, and pay over just and fair compensation for the wrongs I have suffered.

Arthur was dumbfounded. He could not recall the last night he had shared a bed with his own wife, much less with any other woman. Still, the stranger was clearly a man of noble birth, given his expensive armor and weapons. Bearing in mind the rude visitor's high rank, Arthur did his best to respond in a manner that was both respectful and firm:

My Lord, I am sure you are mistaken. I visit the bed of only one woman, my lawfully wedded wife, Queen Guinevere. I assume that you have spoken the way you did because you are suffering from an affliction that has hobbled your reason. Lay down your sword and shield, and let my servants dress you in a fine, soft mantle. I employ the finest healers in all of Britain, and I am sure one of them can restore you to good health. In the meantime, please tell what your name is and who your wife is. I will send out messengers to bring her to you here to comfort you and aid in your recovery.

But the stranger did not lay aside his weapons. His body trembling and his eyes full of hate, he spoke again: Your arrogant words only make your crimes even more outrageous and unforgiveable. My name is Meleagant, prince of Gorre. Guinevere is my wife. Return her to me or defend yourself in a trial by combat.

Arthur now was certain that this man was utterly bereft of his reason and in urgent need of a healer. So he tried again, gently, to bring him around to a sensible course: My Lord Meleagant, you are most welcome here in Camelot. I once fought alongside your father, King Bagdemagus, an excellent knight and an honorable man. You have his bold and daring spirit. As you are a man of such noble lineage, your words must be the result of some unfortunate ailment—maybe a fever of the brain—or perhaps a demon torments your dreams at night. As all the people of Britain know well, Queen Guinevere's father, the good King Leodegrance of Cameliard, gave her hand to me in marriage, with the Round Table as her dowry, in sincere and humble gratitude for my aid in driving the Saxons from his lands. The Bishop of Cameliard performed the betrothal ceremony in the cathedral at Cameliard, in front of hundreds of witnesses. There can be no doubt that Guinevere and I are husband and wife, in the eyes of God and man alike.

But Meleagant continued to press his case: That betrothal was unlawful, as Guinevere had already been given to me. Guinevere's mother had been a dear friend of a wondrous fairy. This fairy had also taken a liking to me when I was a young knight. Overcome by her enchanted beauty, I had sought her hand in marriage. But she refused me: While she had once loved a mortal man, he had betrayed her, and she feared I would be no better. Still, she wished to see me wed to a woman of outstanding beauty and virtue, and thus she prevailed upon her friend, the Queen of Cameliard, to betroth her daughter Princess Guinevere to me. Thus, I had been lawfully engaged to Guinevere before you had ever spoken to her father.

And there is more proof that you are not her rightful husband. For many years now, you have claimed Guinevere as your wife and had free access to her bed. As there is no more beautiful woman in the world, your lusts must have driven you into her arms on many nights. But despite enjoying your Queen's favors for so long, where are your children? You have no son to inherit your crown. You do not even have daughters to marry off. The reason is obvious: Your marriage is unlawful and God, in outraged disgust, has closed up her womb and denied you any issue.

So I say to you again King Arthur: Return my wife Guinevere to me, with fitting and just compensation, and I will graciously forgive your many insults to my honor. If you insist on keeping her, then I challenge you to a trial by combat, where I have every confidence that God will give me the strength to defeat you, as Our Father in Heaven always vindicates the righteous and smites the guilty.

At these words, the knights standing near King Arthur—his nephew Gawain, Kay the Seneschal, Lucan the Butler, Dodinel the Savage, and Sagramore of Hungary—drew their swords and denounced Meleagant as a traitor and a liar who would soon repent of his vicious slanders.

Meleagant, however, did not flinch or reach for his weapons. This knight has no fear, Arthur reflected, a sure sign that he somehow truly believes in his mad cause.

Arthur told his knights to stay their hands and step back. He was wary of shedding the blood of a lord with kinsmen and liegemen who would not hesitate to take up arms and seal off their fortresses in vengeance against the court in Camelot. He recalled only too well the brutal war between his father, Uther Pendragon, and Uther's liegeman, Duke Gorlois, which had nearly destroyed the kingdom of Logres. *He* would not be so foolish or reckless. There must be a way to make peace, but first he needed to persuade Meleagant to cool his boiling blood.

So Arthur tried again: My Lord Meleagant, your words are uttered in haste and anger. But if you use your sober reason, you can clearly perceive the folly in them. If Guinevere was not my lawful wife, then why did her mother not say so when we were betrothed? As you well know, and as I have reminded you again today, our marriage was known to all and celebrated in a Mass sung by the Bishop of Cameliard before hundreds of Britons.

You point to a lack of issue from my marriage. But in this you show a foolish ignorance of God's ways. As is related in holy scripture, our Father Abraham was lawfully wedded to his wife Sarah, but they had no children until Sarah was ninety years old. Indeed, it was when Abraham pretended that Sarah was his sister and passed her off as a harlot to the King of Egypt, that he tempted God's mighty wrath.

I wish no quarrel with you. You and your father and your liegemen have served Logres well and loyally for many years. You should rest now and weigh your words later when you are calm and your mind is at peace. You shall stay here, in my palace, as my honored guest. Surrender your weapons and Sir Kay and Sir Lucan will escort you to your room.

Meleagant's face now flushed red with renewed rage. He drew his sword and demanded justice, then and there, for the outrages that had been visited upon him. He called upon Arthur to take up his weapons without delay and prove in battle the legitimacy of his marriage.

Arthur sighed with growing impatience and signaled to his knights to disarm Meleagant. They promptly descended upon him, took his sword and shield away, and pinned him down on a table while two squires forcibly removed his armor. Arthur then directed Lucan and Kay to escort Meleagant to a room in the palace where he could rest and be tended by a fine and learned healer—under appropriate guard.

II. The Difficulty of Being King

KING ARTHUR HAD hoped that Meleagant would be restored to his reason if he was treated with honor and given time to reflect upon his rash words. But over the next few days, Meleagant remained as stubborn as ever: He continued to insist Guinevere was his lawful wife, and he would not withdraw his demand for a trial by combat to vindicate his rights.

At first, Arthur had sent an expert healer to examine his unwelcome guest. Ever since the death of the wizard Merlin, the court at Camelot had lacked a healer who could harness the full powers of the ancient spirits and fairies of Britain. Nevertheless, the man he sent to Meleagant had assisted Merlin for many years and acquired some of the famed enchanter's wisdom and learning.

As the healer later recounted to Arthur, he had tried to ask Meleagant about his nervous condition, diet, and the state of his dreams. But Meleagant had refused to answer and, instead, berated the healer as a sniveling little peasant sent to shame an honorable knight with a just cause into silence.

Nevertheless, the healer did feel he could make a tentative diagnosis of the patient based upon the way the blood had entered, departed, and then again returned to Meleagant's cheeks; the way he had paced restlessly; and the pattern of his breathing. Drawing upon these careful observations, the healer was confident that a particular mixture of certain herbs and dried berries, cooked at a sufficiently high temperature, would restore Meleagant's reason.

Relieved that there was such a cure, Arthur thanked the healer and ordered the potion to be prepared and blended subtly into the thick venison stew that would be served to Meleagant that evening. Arthur instructed his cook to use generous amounts of salt and ale to flavor the stew so that Meleagant would be unable to taste the medicine that had been cleverly mixed in.

Hopeful that the remedy had worked, the next morning Arthur sent Sir Kay to check upon Meleagant and inquire whether he would withdraw his challenge. But Kay reported back that Meleagant still refused to relent.

So King Arthur tried a different approach. He summoned his household priest and ordered him to hear Meleagant's confession and persuade the headstrong knight to return to reason. After all, Arthur pointed out, the Holy Church had publicly sanctioned and celebrated his marriage to Guinevere, so Meleagant's slanders were directed as much against the Church's honor and good name as his own.

Yet when the priest returned to Arthur later that day, his report was grim: Meleagant had not wavered in his challenge. The only sin he confessed was waiting so long to confront King Arthur. He admitted that he had known for years of Arthur's treachery, but he had been dissuaded from asserting his lawful claim to Guinevere by his father's cowardly counsel and his own craven fears.

He had even been tempted to try to wed another woman. Three times he had been betrothed to a different highborn lady. And three times his bride had been afflicted with a horrible disease—one killed by fever, one deformed by leprosy, and one ruined by a loathsome pox contracted from an illicit lover.

After these failed engagements, Meleagant became convinced that God was punishing him for letting another man fornicate with his lawful wife Guinevere. God was calling upon him to put his faith in the justice and goodness of Heaven and not to fear the ways and arms of mortal men, even the mighty King of Logres in his strong castle at Camelot.

King Arthur was now overcome with despair. If Meleagant's challenge was not answered, then Arthur's vassals would whisper that their King, the famed wielder of the enchanted sword Excalibur, could no longer defend his own honor. He could already hear their words echoing in his mind: Mighty King Arthur knows fear for the first time in his life and shirks away from battle like a cowardly maiden—this can only be because he knows that Meleagant's cause is just.

So perhaps, Arthur's thoughts continued, he should do battle with this madman. But what then? If he should be the victor, then Meleagant's father, brothers, and their vassals would be honor bound to rebel and seek vengeance. Or even if they felt it imprudent to revolt now—for they were not strong enough on their own to resist Camelot—maybe they would seethe quietly for years, nurturing their grievances, until an opportune moment came such as a renewed Saxon invasion of Britain. Then, when he would least expect it, Meleagant's kin would betray him.

The other possible outcome of a trial by combat would be his death. That would plunge Logres into chaos. As there was no legitimate heir sired by Arthur, his barons would turn on each other in a bloody scramble for the throne.

Arthur thus saw no clear way out of his dilemma. How, he wondered, could a powerful King be so easily trapped by one raving lunatic?

Perhaps, his thoughts continued, there *was* something amiss with his betrothal. He stretched his memory back to when he had first met Guinevere, during the wars that had followed upon Uther

Pendragon's death. Arthur's succession to the throne, despite Merlin's support, had been contested, and he had been forced to take the field against several rebellious barons who should have sworn fealty to him.

Guinevere's father, King Leodegrance of Cameliard, had been a faithful vassal of Uther Pendragon. After Uther's death, Merlin had entrusted the Round Table to him for safekeeping during the wars with Arthur's barons. Although Leodegrance had promptly recognized Arthur as the rightful heir to the throne of Logres and never wavered in his loyalty, the Saxons had taken advantage of the chaos in Britain to invade Cameliard and pillage his lands. Leodegrance was badly outnumbered and forced to withdraw behind his castle walls, to which the Saxons laid siege.

When Arthur learned of the danger to his liegeman, he and Marlin led a battalion of knights to Cameliard to relieve the siege. Charging the Saxon camp from behind, taking them by surprise, Arthur's superior cavalry troops quickly routed the invaders and drove them away.

After this victory, the gates of the castle were swung open and Leodegrance rode out to welcome his rescuers. Arthur and Merlin then stayed with him in his palace for the next several weeks. The three men spoke mostly of military matters—how the barons' rebellion was collapsing, where Saxon raiding parties were landing, what supplies of grain, weapons, and horses were necessary for the war campaign, and whether Arthur's maps were accurate.

Meanwhile, Merlin demanded the return of the Round Table to Camelot. He reminded Leodegrance that he had fashioned the enchanted Round Table for Uther Pendragon's court and had only temporarily stowed it in Cameliard. But Leodegrance demurred, expressing his concern over whether the Round Table could be safely transported back to Camelot—perhaps it was better to wait a little while longer, until peace was firmly established throughout the land. Merlin grew angry and accused Leodegrance of underhanded theft, but Leodegrance countered that it might be wiser to spread Logres' magical treasures across several palaces, including, of course, his own.

It was during one of these arguments that Leodegrance had suddenly changed the topic of conversation by jumping to his feet and announcing that his daughter, Princess Guinevere, had come to pay her respects and to thank Arthur for his bravery in battle. Arthur could only vaguely recall this first meeting with his future wife. She was wearing fine and expensive clothes, he was certain of that, but he could not picture the color or the style of her gown. Her thick golden hair fell over her shoulders, he remembered that detail clearly, and she was tightly poised, as if she were presiding over a ceremony at court. Arthur had stiffly thanked her for her praises of his valor and felt relieved when she left the room again.

He did not remember thinking much about Guinevere during the following days. In retrospect, he realized that she must have been around him quite a bit—at feasts, at court, in the palace corridors—but he had no memory of speaking with her, or even noticing her. She had been like one of the rich tapestries hanging on the walls: exceedingly lovely and well-crafted, worth glancing at once and quickly, but nothing terribly urgent or important.

His next memory about Guinevere, in fact, did not involve Guinevere at all. Merlin had come to his bed chamber late one night and asked if he had given any thought to marriage.

Arthur replied that he had not. He confessed he had little interest in women, and found it irksome when his knights wasted their time on love affairs instead of honing their skills with their lances and shields.

Merlin, however, encouraged him to marry: Your Majesty, it is not good for a man to be alone. Your father, Uther Pendragon, also once told me that he had no interest in women and had eyes only for fighting and hunting. But then one day he saw the Lady Igraine—wife of Duke Gorlois—and his desire was enflamed, and his obsession to possess her drove the Duke to rebellion and caused much harm to befall Logres. If Uther had only married earlier and had a woman in his bed to quench his passions before they burst forth like a raging fire, then many good knights would have been saved from a needless death.

And Your Majesty will need an heir, legitimate and clearly recognized, to ensure peace and prosperity for your people.

Arthur coolly weighed Merlin's words and ultimately agreed with his reasoning. But, he asked Merlin, which lady should he marry?

Merlin responded: Which lady has stirred your passion?

Arthur said that none had. While he acknowledged that some ladies were prettier or better mannered than others, he had no preference among them, except that he would prefer someone who would not try to intrude upon his time for hunting or jousting.

Merlin pressed further: But aren't there certain attributes you desire in a lady? Do you like them fair or dark, tall or short, slender or more rounded?

But Arthur merely shrugged his shoulders in response. He had never given the matter much thought.

Then Merlin made a suggestion: Why not marry Princess Guinevere, Leodegrance's daughter? She was pretty, about the right age, and well-mannered. And perhaps Leodegrance would be willing to part with the Round Table as her dowry.

Arthur liked this idea: He also wanted the Round Table back in Camelot and he supposed she would do as well as any other noble lady. And she *was* lovely, which would make it less bothersome to sire an heir upon her.

So Arthur gave Merlin permission to propose the marriage to Leodegrance.

The next morning Arthur rode out beyond the castle walls to confer with his knights in their camp in the surrounding meadow and to inspect the quality of their weapons and armor. Alarmed at the worn-down state of their arms, he hastily summoned the leader of the guild of blacksmiths of Cameliard and arranged for the local smiths to forge the necessary new swords and lances.

By the time he returned to the palace in the middle of the afternoon, Arthur had almost forgotten about his conversation with Merlin from the previous night. He was thus caught off guard when Leodegrance greeted him with a too-familiar embrace and a toast to uniting their two families. Once he had recovered himself, Arthur silently nodded along with the cries of congratulations and the excited babble about plans for the betrothal ceremony.

Merlin added that King Leodegrance had graciously agreed to provide the Round Table as a dowry for Princess Guinevere.

Several days later the betrothal ceremony was held. There must have been hundreds of people in that cathedral, Arthur thought, none of whom had protested that there was anything inappropriate in the proceedings. The bishop of Cameliard performed the rites, showing the Holy Church's unequivocal public approval of the marriage match.

Nevertheless, Arthur recalled being bored by the whole affair. And Guinevere? Arthur did not recall speaking to her. He had looked at her in the beginning when she was trembling with excitement, but by the end she seemed just as listless as he was.

From the cathedral, he had returned to his knights' camp and ridden away toward battles in other parts of Britain. Arthur gave no more thought to his bride until after the fighting had finally ended, when he summoned her to join him in Camelot.

Thinking over these events again he felt reassured that his claim to be Guinevere's lawfully wedded husband was secure and just. If this knight Meleagant should force a trial by combat, Arthur was confident that God would grant him a swift and decisive victory.

III. The Kidnapping

KING ARTHUR WAS awakened in his bed in a most unpleasant manner: A gaggle of half-dressed knights—Kay, Lucan, Gawain, maybe others—had barged into his room, tore aside the canopy of his bed, and were jumping up and down, waving their hands and screaming incoherently.

Once Arthur had wiped the fog of sleep from his eyes and calmed his men down sufficiently to understand what they were saying, he was finally able to grasp the alarming news: Meleagant had ridden away, in the dead of night, with Queen Guinevere as his captive. Sir Kay had been alerted at dawn, when the guards were due to change shifts, that Meleagant had escaped his room and murdered the men who had been posted at his door. And then, to make matters worse, Queen Guinevere's servants had run to Kay to tell him that their lady was nowhere to be found.

Sir Kay now woke Lucan and Gawain and the three investigated further. Meleagant's horse and arms were gone, although the stable hands could not explain how or why. The sentries stationed on the ramparts said that, shortly after the city gates were opened at sunrise, a horse had bolted out of Camelot across the meadow—swift as only a knight's charger could go— and on its back were two figures, a man with a shield around his neck and a woman seated in front of him in the saddle. By the time that the sentries were able to send a messenger out to follow the knight and inquire who he was, the rider and his lady had already disappeared far into the dense forest.

King Arthur thanked his knights for their thoroughness and added that the underhanded treachery of murdering guards by surprise in the dead of night showed clearly that Meleagant was a man with no chivalry or honor. But, Arthur continued, he did not understand how the Queen could have been so easily seized from her own bedroom. How did no one hear her screams? Had her servants been bribed and corrupted? Or drugged?

He ordered that Guinevere's entire household be questioned immediately.

Following their King's instructions, Kay and Lucan promptly corralled an assembly of bleary-eyed and trembling ladies in waiting, servant girls, and guards. Yet each one told the same baffling story: There had been no screams or sounds of any kind.

Could an enchantment have been used to conceal the abduction? King Arthur asked.

Kay responded that there were no traces of unusual herbs, potions, or powders in the Queen's apartments. Nor did any of the servants or ladies in waiting recall any of the other telltale signs of sorcery, such as a sudden unnatural sleep or paralysis of the limbs.

Nevertheless, perceiving no better explanation, Arthur continued to press the point: Were there any rumors that Meleagant had studied necromancy or black magic?

But no one present had ever heard any such rumors. While famous as a knight, and a fierce competitor in tournaments, Meleagant had never been reputed to have the skills or knowledge of a wizard.

Still, Arthur's advisors continued, Meleagant *had* claimed his right to Guinevere based upon a pact with a fairy. If such a fairy were involved, then it followed that such an unchristian and dangerous forest creature could avail herself of magical means to spirit away the Queen in the night. Unable to win the queen through threats and bluster and insults, Meleagant had called upon the aid of the fairy whose mischief lay at the root of this squabble. And she had used her black arts to steal the Queen away from Camelot.

But King Arthur was not convinced that there actually was a wicked fairy at the root of his troubles. To begin with, he had no recollection of Queen Guinevere or her mother having dealings with any fairy.

More to the point, when he had still been alive, the wizard Merlin had never said anything about Guinevere and fairies—and Merlin would have known. Merlin was the son of a fairy father (or some other enchanted forest being similar to a fairy), and he had learned his sorcerer's arts from the fairies. If fairies had been implicated in Guinevere's matrimonial arrangements, then that would have been exactly the sort of thing that Merlin would have known about and dealt with at the time.

Arthur's thoughts continued: If only his seer and wizard were still with him, then he was sure Merlin would have discovered what had really happened the night before and taken the necessary steps to recover the Queen and be rid of this mad fool Meleagant. But Merlin was dead, murdered by his treacherous lover Viviane, damn her to hell.

But if there were no meddling fairies or enchantments, then Arthur could only conclude that Guinevere had been a willing participant in her own abduction. Otherwise, there was no explanation for the lack of any outcry or resistance.

Why would Guinevere do such a thing? Arthur was not sure. He had not yet spoken to her about Meleagant's threats and ravings; he had simply assumed that she would, as a matter of course, back her husband's claim. Indeed, even to have broached the subject and asked her questions would have been giving too much credence to that wretch's lies—after all, why would Arthur bother checking Meleagant's accusations against the Queen's memory of events unless he was worried that there may be some truth in them?

Still, *someone* must have spoken to her about Meleagant's challenge—too many people had witnessed his rude intrusion and wild tirade and people like to talk.

Arthur was forced to admit to himself that he knew little about what went on in his wife's heart. He could not remember the last time they had unburdened their worries and cares to one another. For the past several years, they had only seen and spoken to each other at banquets or tournaments or diplomatic receptions or other events of court life. She had always appeared serene and calm, sure of her regal station and the high regard in which she was held. Arthur mused that he had thought of Guinevere the way he had thought of his left foot: As long as it did what he needed it to do, he paid it no heed.

But he did not want to suggest to his vassals and knights that Guinevere was a traitor who had connived in her own kidnapping—such speculation would either bolster Meleagant's fraudulent claim to be her true husband or force Arthur to respond brutally to the Queen's betrayal—probably by beheading or burning her. None of these possibilities were to his advantage.

In sum, thinking through the matter carefully, King Arthur decided that it was best to chalk up the mysterious circumstances of the Queen's abduction to unchristian fairy witchcraft. And when he at last spoke again, he said exactly that.

Later that day, Arthur summoned his counselors and knights to consider what to do next. He declared that Meleagant's kidnapping of Queen Guinevere was a criminal outrage and treason against the crown. As this offense was personal to the King, he said that he was duty bound to ride himself to Meleagant's castle to fight for Guinevere's freedom.

As Arthur had secretly hoped, his men begged him not to place his life in danger in single combat—should he be killed or wounded, the risk to the Kingdom of Logres would be too great— the succession to the throne could be placed in the gravest doubt, leading to war among the barons—or the rich lands of Britain could be exposed to the pillaging of Saxons or Irishmen or worse.

Very well, my lords, Arthur replied, I shall heed your heartfelt pleas, follow your counsel, and remain at Camelot. But then a champion must ride forth on my behalf to reclaim the Queen from her kidnapper.

King Arthur looked around his wide hall, but the many eyes around him turned to the floor to avoid meeting his gaze. Meleagant was famous as a valiant and powerful knight; his fortress at Gorre was strong and could only be reached by perilous crossings. And, to make matters even more fearsome, fairy magic could be aiding him. Hence Arthur was not surprised when the Knights of the Round Table displayed no eagerness for this adventure.

But then Sir Lancelot came forward and boldly offered to ride off at once and make Meleagant pay dearly for his outrageous crimes against the most beautiful, the most virtuous, and the most justly lauded lady in all Christendom. Lancelot swore he would either return victorious, with the Queen vindicated and her honor restored, or the wretched vermin crawling about in that castle in Gorre would have to find a way to remove his head from his neck.

King Arthur did not know Lancelot well. He had only recently joined the court at Camelot. He hailed from Benoic— King Ban's boy, raised by a local fairy on an island in a lake after King Claudas had cut Ban to pieces in a battle. When Lancelot had grown to be a man, the fairy had given him armor, weapons, and a horse and dispatched him to Logres. After jousting well in a couple of tournaments, Arthur had agreed to give him a place at court. Lancelot had been dispatched on several humdrum missions—

beating tax payments out of miserly burghers or knocking the heads of rebellious peasants, things like that—but nothing where the realm's honor was so deeply at stake. Still, better a Lancelot with fire in his blood to rescue the Queen than a more seasoned knight being forced to go against his will, who would abandon the adventure at the slightest obstacle.

But Arthur could not rid himself of the concern that Lancelot was too inexperienced to go forth alone. Thus, after thanking Lancelot for stepping forward as the Queen's champion and praising his bravery and chivalry, King Arthur also directed ten other knights and as many squires to accompany Lancelot on his journey and aid him as he saw fit.

Lancelot protested: This was *his* adventure, and *his* dread oath to liberate the finest woman the world had known since Our Savior Jesus Christ's perfect Virgin Mother or to forfeit his life in the attempt. Such adventures, which render a knight either a great hero or a maggot-filled corpse, could not be shared. Any glory, and any shame, must be his alone.

Arthur tried to get the young knight to see reason: My Lord Lancelot, he said, you have spent too much time listening to the bards' foolish songs. The realm of Gorre is ruled from a strong castle. The terrain is treacherous—many knights before you have become lost in those lands and never returned. You will need the help of able men. There is no shame in that. When I rode out to do battle in my youth, I was accompanied by the enchanter Merlin. And many heroic knights, young and old, also rode with me, shoulder to shoulder. You are a bold knight, and you will one day be a great champion. But I do not want your life, or the Queen's, lost on account of overweening pride.

Lancelot's face clouded over with rage. He began to speak, but then stopped himself. He grinded his teeth, breathed heavily, and looked at the ground.

Then Sir Gawain spoke up and seconded the King's wise counsel. The other knights and noblemen followed in due course too with their firm and considered agreement.

Appearing calmer now, Lancelot glanced up again and begged the King's pardon. It was, he said, his passionate devotion to the cause of the Queen, and his seething anger at the abominable rogue who had dared to dishonor her, that had clouded his reason. But he now recognized the benefit of having other knights to aid and support him in this adventure.

King Arthur stood up and warmly embraced Lancelot. Logres, he said, has been blessed by Almighty God to have knights such as you in her service. Go to your bed and rest; Sir Kay and Sir Lucan will see to all the necessary preparations. You ride for Gorre at dawn.

At these words, the assembly broke into cheers, and then King Arthur gave leave to each man to go his separate way.

IV. The Heavy Heart of the King

AFTER SEEING LANCELOT off at dawn the next morning, Arthur decided to distract himself from his troubles with petitions and lawsuits—tedious and time-consuming bickering over property boundary lines, and legal title to herds of sheep, and whatnot. But when Arthur tried to go to sleep that night, he was beset by a twitching nervousness that would not let him rest. Eventually he wandered downstairs to his empty hall. By the light of a dim candle, he gazed at the tapestries on the walls that depicted the military victories of his youth. Yet those days seemed so far gone that they might have belonged to the memories of a different man.

He put the candle down on a table and sat himself down in an old wooden chair. He missed Queen Guinevere. Which was odd, he thought, because he usually did not take any particular joy in her presence. He wondered if she missed him; he was not sure.

Arthur recalled his wedding night. It had been delayed for a long time because after the betrothal he and Merlin had immediately left Cameliard to engage his enemies elsewhere in Britain. Those wars did not conclude for two years, maybe a little longer. After he had returned triumphant to Camelot, Arthur sent for Guinevere. This was not out of any passion or yearning—after all, he had not bothered writing her any letters or having her portrait drawn for a locket around his neck—but to establish his now reunited Kingdom of Logres on a stable, peaceful basis. For this, he needed a Queen and the expectation that worthy, legitimate heirs to the throne would be forthcoming from her most noble belly.

The wedding took place in the Church of St. Stephen in Camelot. It was exactly what Arthur felt was needed to cement confidence in his rule: a large crowd cheering, clapping, and crying tears of joy, rose petals strewn about the aisles, a wizened old priest with a booming voice, and the bride: tall and graceful in a white silk gown and veil. The feast afterwards was full of music and dancing and acrobats and jugglers. A traveling bard even sang poems lauding young Arthur's already famous victories on the battlefield.

And at the end of that truly wondrous day (which was after a wait of more than two years from the betrothal ceremony in Cameliard), Arthur knew that he and Guinevere were to spend the night together. He had not given much thought to this last task. Older, married men had always told him that their wedding nights were sublime pleasures, so Arthur simply assumed that, once things started in between the bed sheets, he would have no difficulty in completing his conjugal duty.

When he entered Guinevere's room that night, she was sprawled over the bed on top of the blankets. In the dim, smoky light, he could see she was wearing nothing but a flimsy, garishly red shift; her long blonde hair was loose and wild. Her head was tilted playfully to the side, and her lips were slightly parted in an inviting smile.

Yet all that beauty did not cause him to feel anything, save— perhaps—the admiration he had always felt for the striking marble statues in the crumbling, abandoned Roman villas scattered about Britain. He realized only too well that he was not feeling what he was supposed to feel in the presence of a half-naked beautiful woman writhing atop luxurious sheets.

Still, he tried. He undressed, grabbed her boldly, and imitated the gestures of passionate love. For a while, he thought he was doing a passable job of it. But when the time came to do what was necessary to sire an heir, his body simply could not muster the excitement needed to complete the deed.

Guinevere looked disappointed at first, but then she brightened up and said that Arthur must be exhausted from such a busy day and that perhaps another night, when the day had been less taxing, would be better. She squeezed his hand, kissed his cheek, and nuzzled against his side. Once she had fallen into a deep sleep, Arthur left her and returned to his own room.

The next several weeks were more of the same: Arthur just could not complete his duties as a husband—somehow, he could not muster the hot-blooded lusts other men experienced so naturally with their ravishing young wives. He felt embarrassed and foolish, and he avoided Guinevere's company.

The Queen did her best to help him. She wore alluring garments, scented her body with seductive oils, and painted her lips and eyes with sensuous reds and purples. She even tried various different acts beforehand to rouse Arthur's passion.

But nothing worked. Soon Guinevere's face mirrored the resignation and despair in her husband's heart. When Arthur would approach her bed at night, she wore the expression of a sick patient bracing herself to swallow an apothecary's bitter medicine. There were often tracks of dried tears on her face, and Arthur knew how much his failures as a husband were causing Guinevere to suffer. But this knowledge only deepened his loathing of her presence.

In desperation, Arthur finally turned to Merlin. For a long time, he had been too proud to seek help for his marital difficulties. But he realized that matters could not continue in this way. Logres needed an heir, and he needed a marriage that did not weaken or dishonor him.

Merlin nodded thoughtfully as Arthur described his troubles. Then the little sorcerer, who never failed him, brewed a potion of foul-smelling weeds and bark and told Arthur to drink it three times a day for the next three days. And then approach the Queen's bed.

Merlin's cure worked: Arthur was at last able to take Queen Guinevere's maidenhood and to do what was necessary to sire an heir. The next morning, she joined him for breakfast, full of smiles and giggles and blushes. Arthur's burden of shame was lifted from his heart, and he walked confidently again about his palace and courtyard.

For several blissful months, Arthur visited Guinevere's bed regularly and did what needed to be done. Guinevere now shone radiantly—she enjoyed being held and loved, he noticed, and she now carried herself with an arrogant, easy pride in her own beauty.

But Arthur was still troubled. While Merlin's potion had fixed his body—like straightening a broken axle in a wagon—his soul still felt no rapture in Guinevere's arms and nothing she did aroused any passion in him. His joy was entirely in driving away his earlier afflictions of guilt and embarrassment—the joy of executing a duty well and with dignity.

And then a new difficulty arose: Guinevere failed to conceive a child. For King Arthur, the whole point of having a wife and spending nights in her bed was to sire heirs to the throne who would guarantee a legitimate succession and inspire confidence in the ruling dynasty. But despite his body finally doing its appropriate part, the Queen's womb remained stubbornly shut.

So Arthur turned back to Merlin, who brewed more foul-smelling potions from boiled weeds and roots, which Guinevere dutifully swallowed down for the next few months. Merlin promised the King that a tiny Prince of Logres would soon be on the way.

But this time the wizard's remedy did not work. Merlin tried a couple of different mixtures—assuring the royal couple that the spell needed only a slight tweaking, a little more of one herb and a little less of another—yet none of the concoctions he brewed could open up Guinevere's womb.

Merlin investigated the matter further. He drew up detailed horoscopes for the King and the Queen and then went deep into the forest, inside a hollow tree trunk, to give himself up to visions and prophecies. When he was finished, his report to Arthur was grim: Guinevere was fated to be barren all of her days. The only way to ensure a stable succession was to divorce Guinevere and find a new bride.

Arthur's heart sank at this news. He recalled only too clearly how difficult it had been to perform his marital duties with Guinevere, despite her youth and ravishing beauty. To go through the same ordeal, with a new and probably far less lovely wife, filled him with dread. He never wanted to feel such shame again.

He asked Merlin if perhaps there was some ambiguity in the movement of the stars or the prophetic visions. Perhaps Merlin had been forced to interpret equivocal signs, and the ultimately correct interpretation could be different.

But Merlin shook his head. He was certain: The Queen's womb was a desert in which nothing could bloom.

Arthur then spoke with his confessor at St. Stephen's Church and described his troubles and Merlin's prophecy. What counsel could the Church offer?

The priest replied that Merlin was a vile pagan and a deceiver, whose dark magic derived from his father being a demon. While Merlin could perceive certain matters beyond the ken of mortal men, he ultimately failed to see the whole truth because he could not grasp the grace and mercy of the One True God and His Son

Who had died to redeem all mankind. All things were possible for a man who puts his trust in the Christian faith. As we are taught in the Book of Genesis, Sarah's womb was closed until she was ninety years old, when she bore Isaac.

Encouraged by the priest's words, Arthur redoubled his commitment to Christianity. He and Guinevere heard Mass and received communion each day. They were both confessed several times each week. And so that the Christian God could not fail to be moved by Arthur's zeal and devotion, he built innumerable new churches and abbeys throughout Britain.

But Guinevere still failed to conceive a child.

Arthur resigned himself to his fate. He went to church less and less. He stopped visiting Guinevere's bed, or even discussing the issue of children with her. Instead, they would meet in the morning for breakfast and discuss their duties for the day. With his mind no longer focused on siring heirs, the King now noticed how shrewd a counselor Guinevere was. Her advice on noble alliances, foreign embassies, and thorny legal disputes proved wise and helpful. Arthur had at last become truly enamored of the Queen, but as a fellow administrator of the kingdom.

And he thought she was happy. She was respected, admired, and obeyed. He watched her preside with a tranquil and affable grace over the ladies of the court. When the King and Queen were seated together, on their thrones or in the stands in a tournament, Arthur thought they cut a splendid figure and inspired confidence in his rule.

Men fell over themselves in praising Guinevere's beauty, stealing many fleeting, lustful, hungry glances at her person. Far from arousing any jealousy, these displays of desire for the Queen made Arthur feel he was a mighty king; lesser men envied his greatness—his vast lands, his sumptuous palace, his magical sword Excalibur, his peerless horses, and his beautiful wife. Guinevere's beauty, which he encouraged her to flaunt at every opportunity, was another sign of God's grace and blessing upon Logres—yet more proof that King Arthur was no ordinary man.

But parading the beautiful Queen Guinevere as a sign of divine favor had now become a weakness: With her kidnapping, Arthur worried that there were now speculations, even if still hushed and furtive, that God may have withdrawn His favor from Logres and its sovereign. For another man to display Guinevere on his balcony would be to show that God had transferred His blessings to a new champion.

If only Merlin was still here, he sighed to himself, he would have known what to do—what bit of sorcery would have brought the Queen back, or stricken Meleagant and his household with a plague of boils on their flesh.

But Merlin was dead, and King Arthur would have to trust in Sir Lancelot. At least Lancelot appeared steadfast, and he certainly expressed an ardent devotion to the Queen.

Such were Arthur's thoughts as the sleepless hours of the moonless black night slowly dripped away.

V. Lancelot Triumphant

WEEKS PASSED. SLEEP continued to evade Arthur, and nothing in his palace, it seemed to him, was ever in the right place—everywhere he turned, he would see that a cup, or a wine barrel, or a curtain, was not where he thought it should be, he would feel his fury rise, and he would unleash a torrent of abuse at whatever servant was nearest to him at that moment.

Nor did he trust his knights and courtiers any longer. He was sure that he could hear whispered conversations all around him, but when he would turn a sharp corner in a passageway, the hushed discussions would suddenly change into stiff, theatrically grave greetings—greetings of the kind, Arthur thought, that distant relations give to mourners at a funeral. He heard pity in those greetings—pity for the cuckold who was too feeble to hold onto his treasure of a beautiful wife.

There was a thin line, his thoughts continued, between pity and treason: If the King could be pitied, he could be looked down upon. If he could be looked down upon, he could be dispensed with and tossed aside. No one rallied to the banner of a weakling.

He reflected further: Except for Lancelot, his knights, liegemen who held vast estates and well-fortified castles as fiefdoms from him, had all declined to take up his cause and rescue

Guinevere. At the time he had assumed that they were merely cowards, but maybe there was not such a benign explanation. The loss of Guinevere would show that Arthur was no longer blessed as Heaven's favorite; that could be an opportunity for a man with dangerous ambitions. Maybe his knights had hesitated to aid their lord because they saw in his distress a chance to usurp the throne for themselves.

Arthur finally concluded that he could only trust Sir Kay the Seneschal, whose habit of insulting other knights had rendered him distinctly unpopular, if not outright despised, and thus uniquely dependent upon King Arthur's favor and protection.

Arthur instructed Kay to have his pages and servants eavesdrop and report on conversations amongst Camelot's knights.

Soon Kay was providing Arthur with a steady stream of garbled excerpts from overhead conversations whose meaning was maddeningly unclear. After all, when two knights bantered about how they would set their hunting dogs upon a boar in the woods, were they speaking of a hunt or speaking of the King, the old feeble pig ready now to be slaughtered?

He would turn these reports over in his mind, and his confused thoughts drove sleep even further from his eyes. He found it difficult to follow the thread of discussions or petitions. His courtiers would be forced to gently remind His Majesty of all sorts of pertinent details that kept slipping his mind, leading Arthur to grow angry, convinced as he was that these supposedly helpful prompts were offered in the spirit of ridicule and contempt—another sly attempt to diminish his honor.

And there was no word from Lancelot. Arthur had sent several messengers to ride out after him and his party to check on their progress and report back, but all anyone could say was that Lancelot had ridden hard, with almost no rest, and had disappeared past the borders of Logres deep into Gorre.

Arthur would then sigh and dismiss the messengers. Perhaps, he mused, the wicked barons who sought to usurp his throne had corrupted the messengers with gold, and he was being told just enough lies to give him false hope until the traitors were ready to strike their blow and sever his head from his neck.

Or maybe Lancelot had betrayed him, too. Arthur's thoughts were a mad jumble: Lancelot was in league with Meleagant and had betrayed him to serve the lords of Gorre. Or Lancelot was in league with the would-be usurpers of the throne of Logres and had no intention to liberate the Queen; all the better to show Arthur's pathetic impotence and the loss of his divine election to the kingship. Or maybe Lancelot himself sought the throne and would seek to woo Guinevere to his cause by saving her and then poisoning her mind with malicious words about how her husband had been too cowardly to carry off the rescue himself.

But these frenzied, jumbled speculations finally ended when one evening. As the sun was setting, Lancelot arrived back in Camelot and returned Queen Guinevere to her lawful husband. Never before, Arthur thought, had there been such a rosy color in her cheeks and such joy—almost girlish, giggling joy—in her smiles.

Sir Lancelot also handed to Arthur a wooden stick with its top covered by a linen sack, which gave off a hideous stench. Lancelot smirked and kindly asked Sir Kay to remove the sack and uncover the fine trophy underneath—a special gift worthy of a great king.

When Kay removed the covering, Arthur beheld Meleagant's severed head, rotting away, with slimy maggots crawling about and nibbling at its blankly staring eyeballs, mounted on the end of the stick. Feeling as if a terrible weight had been suddenly lifted from his heart, Arthur laughed long and hard and ordered the head to be mounted on the castle ramparts so that all Camelot and the surrounding countryside could bear witness to the fate of any arrogant knight who would dare to dishonor the mighty King of Logres—the man whom God Himself had truly and unquestionably chosen to be the ruler of Britain.

Arthur ordered that there be a banquet held later that night in honor of the Queen's rescue and safe return home. However, feeling exhausted after so many tense sleepless nights mulling over his earlier, unfounded fears of treason, he now retired alone to his bed to sleep before the feast. He considered speaking to Guinevere in private and asking how she had fared in Meleagant's castle, but then he quickly decided that she, like him, must also be terribly tired and in need of rest. And, anyway, she looked so happy—why ruin her good cheer by dredging up what were no doubt painful memories of her captivity? There would be a time for that later. Yes, let her remain at the moment in that warm joyful glow of her safe homecoming.

Later that evening, after a lavish banquet of deliciously spiced roast pork washed down by the best wines in the royal cellar, King Arthur asked Sir Lancelot to recount his adventures to the court at Camelot and tell how he had triumphed over the wicked Meleagant and restored the Queen to her rightful place in the palace.

But when Lancelot stood up to speak, his words were drowned out by raucous cheering and the loud banging of goblets on the table. Arthur reclined in his seat and smiled; the strong wine and the gentle orange candlelight had pleasantly dulled his senses. He leaned over to say something to Guinevere, who was seated next to him, but then he noticed that her eyes were fixed in an intense, trembling stare at Sir Lancelot. She was blushing and smiling—she had that expression of freshly ripened love that Arthur had sometimes seen on the faces of happy brides at other men's weddings. Arthur looked back over to Lancelot; he saw how the young knight was tall, broad-shouldered, with a handsome, manly face. For a fleeting moment, Arthur mused that Guinevere and Lancelot would make a lovely bride and groom.

Once the noise had finally died down, Lancelot addressed himself to Arthur: Your Majesty, My Lord King Arthur, I humbly thank you for this rich feast and for your generous hospitality. But even more, I thank you for having granted me the honor of riding forth as your champion to fight on behalf of the Queen. I know only too well how Your Majesty's blood boiled with righteous fury at the insult done to the honor of your loving and faithful wife, and how eager you were to seize your arms, ride after the criminal Meleagant, and run him through with your lance. But out of great love and pity for your many vassals in Logres, who feared that their sovereign, upon whom alone their entire happiness depends, would be in mortal danger in the foreign lands of treacherous Gorre, Your Majesty reluctantly agreed to appoint a champion to act in your stead. And although I am but a young knight who has yet to win wide renown, you chose me—you had faith that I would be a true and loyal knight, and that I would fight to the very death to bring back Queen Guinevere to Camelot.

For the stakes in this adventure were grave. We have all been blessed to live under the wise and kind guidance of our noble Queen Guinevere, the finest lady in all Christendom—no, the finest lady in all the world, damn any heathen whore who would dare compare herself to our Queen. Her beauty, her grace, and her unwavering Christian faith have inspired us to mighty feats in battle and to incline towards justice and mercy in times of peace. Logres without the light of Her Majesty Queen Guinevere would be like the Earth without the light of the Sun. With Her Majesty abducted and taken far away from us, I am sure we all trembled with the fear that God's favor and blessing had left our land.

As soon as it was daylight, I rode out from the gates of Camelot toward Meleagant's stronghold in the land of Gorre. I heard the peasants and the monks cheering me as I passed by on my charger, urging me on in my quest, but I did not slow down to thank them and bless them, as perhaps I ought to have done in keeping with the customs of chivalry and courtliness. But elegant manners and easy praises be damned: I had to save the Queen. Any delay meant one more horrible moment of Her Majesty suffering miserably in the sweaty, filthy hands of that degenerate kidnapper.

I fought off the temptations of sleep and forced myself to keep riding, never stopping, all through the night. By sunrise the next morning, I had arrived at the borders of Gorre. I was now alone. The knights and squires who were to accompany me had not ridden as fast as I did, and they must have stopped somewhere along the road to sleep and rest. No matter: I had always sought to achieve this adventure on my own.

The passage into Gorre is steep and deadly. There is a narrow road winding dangerously along the ledge of a deep ravine, with jagged boulders and vicious wolves at the bottom—any slip of the foot meant certain death.

I spurred my charger forward but proceeded slowly and cautiously. The Sun beat down harshly, and the sweat from my forehead soaked the inside of my helmet. I felt lightheaded and dizzy, but nevertheless I knew I had to push forward for the sake of the Queen.

Then I felt something give way beneath me—my horse's legs had buckled, and he tumbled down the side of the ravine to his death. I would have fallen to my death, too, if I had not been fortunate enough to be near an overhanging tree branch, which my hand caught just in time—may Our Lord and Savior Jesus Christ and His Holy Virgin Mother be praised and thanked for rescuing me from disaster.

With tremendous effort I managed to pull myself back up onto the path. But what I now saw made my heart shudder: a huge writhing serpent, breathing foul, thick fumes and baring long vicious fangs dripping with venom.

The monster lunged at me. I jumped away and grabbed the same branch again, lowering myself down the side of the ravine and unsheathing my sword. I waited for the monster to slither its way toward me, hissing and groaning, staring at me with its immense hideous yellow eyes. When its head was close enough that I could smell its poisonous breath, I swung my sword quickly and madly, not fully sure of my aim until I heard a banging and a falling and watched the giant serpent's severed head and lifeless body tumble down into bottom of the ravine and shatter against the rocks.

Then I pulled myself back up onto the road. I felt weak and sick from the serpent's noxious breath and fell down to my knees. I unlaced my helmet and tried to steady myself with the fresh air. But it was no use—there was too much poison in my veins, and I was sure I would soon be dead.

But once more God in His Great and Abiding Love came to my aid: I vomited repeatedly until all the putrid toxin had been expelled from my flesh. When I was at last finished purging myself, I struggled hard to stand back up and walk on. Feeble as I was then, I was fortunate not to encounter another foe, human or monster, on that narrow ledge.

As dusk fell, I reached the end of the ravine and found a broad highway. I sat down on a tree stump to rest and, with any luck, await a passing Christian who could offer me the charity of food and shelter, and direct my steps toward Meleagant's castle.

It was already night when someone finally came along—a very short, very fat man with a tangled beard driving a horse tethered to an empty cart. I could make out, even in the dim moonlight, that there were words in Latin painted on the cart's sides—"Murderer" and "Thief" and "Ravisher" and "Traitor." It was a cart for hauling criminals through the countryside and the villages, so they could be insulted and humiliated on their way to their just punishment for their terrible crimes.

I stood up, hailed the little man, and asked where a weary traveler could find a crust of bread, a drop of water, and a pile of straw on which to rest his aching bones.

He stopped his horse and silently looked me over. Then he spoke, in a voice brimming with malevolent spite and overweening arrogance: Oh my great and gracious lord, mighty Sir Stranger with No Name, it appears that you have not had an easy stroll across the ravine. You seem a bit worse for the wear. I can perhaps share some hard cheese and wine, but tell me, which way are you heading?

I replied as courteously as I could: My good sir, I seek the castle of Meleagant, knight and prince of these lands.

He frowned and looked at me suspiciously. Leaning forward he spoke again: You are armed like a knight, but your shield is one I have never seen before—those are not the arms of a knight of Gorre. You are a foreigner. Are you King Arthur's messenger boy, sent here to beg Lord Meleagant to please kindly return the lovely Guinevere to Logres? You should know your mission is in vain. Meleagant is deeply in love with his new bride, and I cannot see how she could long resist the charms of a handsome and powerful knight like him. At this very moment, they are no doubt playing with each other, like ardent lovers do, in a sumptuous pavilion spread out on a fine meadow. Why don't you go home, foreigner, and tell your king that he should never have stolen Meleagant's betrothed?

My heart pounded with rage at these vile attacks upon Queen Guinevere's honor—no honest and true Christian could dispute that there is not a more faithful wife in all the world, from misty Thule to the highest mountain peaks of India, than Her Majesty Queen Guinevere. I reached for my sword, fully prepared to teach this nasty little peasant a lesson about slandering the good name of highborn ladies.

I must have scared him because he suddenly changed his tune: Sir knight, he said, I beg your pardon if I have given you cause for insult. Here, have some food and drink.

He handed me a round of hard cheese and a flask of wine. I thanked him, and then ate and drank it all down quickly.

When I was finished, I looked back at the little peasant. He had a devilish grin on his face. My good sir knight, he said, I will happily take you to the gates of the castle of Lord Meleagant. But as you can see, there is only one seat on my cart, and I am already in it, and there is only one horse, and I am already driving him. So I am afraid I cannot help you unless you are willing to ride inside the cart.

I was outraged at this insult—to ride in that prisoner's cart, to be paraded about as if I were some thief or worse—the shame, the disgrace. But I knew that my honor was worth nothing if it should permit the disgusting Meleagant to force his revolting presence upon the beautiful Guinevere for even one more minute than absolutely necessary. So I jumped into the cart and told the haughty little coachman to drive me straightaway to Meleagant's castle. He snickered and whipped the horse, and off we went.

I soon fell asleep.

I awoke when I felt pieces of rotted fruit pelting my head. With the sun high in the sky, I sat up and saw that we were passing through a large town. Peasants and merchants, lowborn men, were screaming insults at me. They laughed at my humiliation and spoke of how this proud lord wasn't so mighty anymore in the prisoner's cart.

I considered leaping out of the cart and severing some of these cackling heads from their miserable bodies. But then I thought: How would taking revenge upon a horde of imbecile serfs alleviate the sufferings of the good Queen Guinevere? I reminded myself that nothing mattered save *her* honor, *her* dignity, *her* happiness. Compared to her, I was as lowly as these disgusting fools—no, worse, I was as lowly as a slimy maggot wriggling inside the belly of a dog's carcass.

So instead of vindicating my own honor, I closed my eyes and prayed to my Savior, God's only begotten son of a virgin mother, Our Lord Jesus Christ, to give me the strength to endure this ordeal as He had endured His ordeal of humiliation during His Holy Passion.

We passed through several towns like this one on the road to Meleagant's castle. But through it all, God gave me the fortitude to persevere and to remain focused on my quest to free Her Majesty Queen Guinevere from her cruel captivity.

The rude imp who drove the cart tossed me on the ground when we at last reached the castle. Before I had the chance to pay him back properly, he had disappeared again down the highway. But the little peasant was no longer my concern. I was now near the Queen and close to freeing her.

Meleagant's castle is situated at the top of a steep hill. The front of the fortress faced the upward tilting slope; the back and the sides were protected by sheer cliffs overlooking rocky gorges. After dusting myself off, I walked up the incline toward the gates. Although my body was stiff from lying in the cart for such a long time, the thought of how the most beautiful and faithful Guinevere was suffering at the hands of a lecherous rogue fired my blood with rage and gave me renewed vigor.

There was no moat or drawbridge. Instead, a giant sat at the entrance—the monster must have been as tall as four knights stacked on top of one another—picking at his enormous black teeth and humming to himself.

I greeted him courteously in the name of God and King Arthur, and kindly requested entry to deliver a message from my lord and sovereign to Prince Meleagant.

The giant answered me just like the base wretch that he was: Sir Whoever-You-Are, I do not care about your God, your Jesus, your Mary, your king, or any of your nonsense. My master is occupied at the moment having his pleasure with your pretty Queen Guinevere and does not wish to be bothered. Go take your message somewhere else.

I again demanded to be admitted into the castle.

The giant now stood up to his full height and picked up his heavy club. He told me again to be gone.

I drew my sword. I offered him one last chance to let me through peacefully; otherwise, he would forfeit his life for his arrogance.

The giant laughed and swung his club at me. I ducked, ran between his legs, and jumped onto the backside of his right calf. The giant yelled all sorts of curses and tried to shake me off of his leg, but my grip was firm. Holding fast to his greasy hairs, I climbed up to the soft flesh behind his knee, and then hacked away with my sword until his leg was severed in two.

The giant fell to the ground screaming in pain. I seized my chance: I ran up to his chest and drove my sword deep into his heart, killing him instantly.

With the giant defeated, I now walked through the castle gates with ease. I strode up to Meleagant's palace and burst into his hall, where I found his vassals swilling wine in their pretty womanly mantles.

I greeted them loudly in the name of Our Savior Jesus Christ and His Majesty King Arthur of Logres.

They all turned their heads and looked at me standing there in my armor, sword in hand, covered in dripping tracks of the giant's freshly spilled blood. Their faces went pale, and their rich goblets fell from their delicate hands to the ground.

One man, even more elegantly dressed than the others, nervously returned my greeting and politely asked how he could be of service to a wandering knight, who had clearly traveled far and undergone terrible adventures and struggles.

I replied that I was an envoy from King Arthur and wished to speak at once with Prince Meleagant.

The well-dressed nobleman ordered a page to find their lord and tell him that an envoy from Kingdom of Logres had arrived. In the meantime, I was invited to refresh myself with wine, fruit, and bread.

About an hour later, two new men entered the hall: The criminal himself, Meleagant, and an old man dressed in fine ermine and sable, who offered me a friendly smile. This old man introduced himself as Bagdemagus, King of Gorre and father of Meleagant. King Bagdemagus greeted me courteously in the name of God and asked what message I brought from King Arthur.

I responded boldly: My Lord, thank you for your kind greeting, and may He Who was born of a virgin and died to redeem us send many blessings upon your land. I have been dispatched to this castle by His Majesty King Arthur of Logres to demand the immediate return of Her Majesty Queen Guinevere, who was treacherously seized from his palace at Camelot. If you will not agree to release the Queen into my custody, then I shall stand as Arthur's champion to fight your son, Prince Meleagant, in a trial by combat for the right to possess her.

Bagdemagus did not directly answer me, but rather pointed out that my armor was stained with freshly spilled blood and asked if I would relate my adventures on the road from Camelot to Gorre.

I gladly did so, omitting nothing. The old king trembled when I told him how I had vanquished both the monstrous serpent and the insolent giant. And I was clear that I could never have mustered such valor or bravery, but for my unwavering devotion to the greatest lady in Christendom, Her Majesty Queen Guinevere. I swore that I would serve her steadfastly until God in Heaven should choose to rend my soul from my flesh.

After hearing my tale, King Bagdemagus assured me that Queen Guinevere had not been mistreated or dishonored in any way. He had expressly forbidden his son from taking his pleasure with the Queen until his claim to her hand had been settled. He was also quick to add that he had not known beforehand that Meleagant had intended to seize Her Majesty by force.

Bagdemagus said that only Meleagant could decide whether he wished to surrender Guinevere or to fight for her hand. But he, Bagdemagus, nevertheless strongly urged his son to relinquish the Queen, noting that my triumphs over the serpent and the giant showed that God was aiding me in my quest.

But Meleagant refused to surrender the most noble and faithful lady, whom he still insisted, in his wickedness, upon calling his rightful bride. He scoffed at my victories, saying that God had preserved me intact only so that Meleagant himself could vindicate his claim to the Queen in fair and public combat.

Bagdemagus begged his son to reconsider, but Meleagant would not relent. However, the king did swear to me that he would abide by the result of our battle: Because I had brought my challenge openly, with no treachery or deceit, and because, if I won, God would have found my cause to be just, Bagdemagus vowed that if his son died in combat, then he would forbid his kinsmen and vassals from taking revenge or hindering our safe passage home to Logres.

I thanked King Bagdemagus for his courtesy and chivalry and asked when we could fight.

He replied that I would first be given an opportunity to rest, bathe, and select fresh arms and a new horse. The trial by combat would be set for the next morning, at the hour of prime, in the flat meadow at the bottom of the hill.

I protested that this delay was unnecessary, and that I was ready to joust that very instant—just give me a horse and a lance, I said, and I will vindicate Queen Guinevere's honor right now.

Bagdemagus replied that I had a great knightly spirit, but he still insisted I be refreshed before the battle—he did not want it said that he had unfairly favored his son by denying King Arthur's champion a chance to recover his strength after an exhausting journey.

And so I was disarmed and forced against my will to spend the day bathing and sleeping in a soft sable robe.

The next morning, I woke well before the hour of prime, when the sky was still dark. I donned the fresh armor that had been provided to me, grabbed a new lance and shield from the hall, and found a horse to my liking in the stables. I rode the beast down to the meadow to await the battle.

As the sun rose, Meleagant came to meet me, fully armed. His father and a crowd of vassals followed him to watch the combat. And, wondrously, standing next to King Bagdemagus I beheld a sight even brighter than the dawning red sun: Her Majesty the Queen in a white gown, tall, proud, and shimmering in her beauty. She deigned to cast a smile down upon me. That one smile gave me the strength of a thousand knights.

We lowered our lances and charged hard at each other. Both spears shattered to bits against our shields, and we were thrown from our horses. We stood right back up, drew our swords and rushed at each other. The sword battle continued for a long time, past the hour of terce. Our shields were hacked to pieces and our hauberks were rent apart by the repeated blows. Finally, I overcame the criminal, took his sword, and knocked him to the ground. I removed his helmet and offered him mercy if he would voluntarily surrender the Queen into my custody.

But he refused and still insisted he was her rightful husband.

King Bagdemagus rushed over to his son lying beaten on the ground and begged him to let go of Guinevere. God has passed judgment, he said. Do not be so proud as to defy the will of

Heaven. Submit to the outcome of the trial by combat and then repent of your sins.

But Meleagant would not relent, no matter how desperate his father's pleas. At last, the King of Gorre stood up again and told me to do what I must do as the victor whose opponent had refused mercy.

And so I cut off Meleagant's head. His father gave it to me as a trophy—he did not want such a shameful son buried in his family's chapel. Mount his head on Camelot's ramparts, he said to me, as an example to those who would put their pride above God's judgment.

The Queen was then immediately delivered into my protection, and I am pleased to report that she was unharmed and had been well cared for. After brief preparations for the journey, we returned to Logres. As we approached the border, we met the party of knights and squires who had been sent to accompany me, but whom I had long ago left behind. They had gotten lost, and apparently had some fighting with the locals – However, nothing too serious.

Lancelot then abruptly sat back down, looking quite satisfied with his tale.

Now King Arthur rose and spoke: God be praised! And may we all rejoice at the bravery and knightly skill shown by Sir Lancelot. In reward for his gallant and daring service, I shall enfeoff Lancelot with a strong fortress and rich lands. I shall also have the finest smiths in Logres forge him new arms, and he may choose any horse in my stable to have as his own. For Sir Lancelot has well merited such honors, and much more besides. The light cast by the sun above us had dimmed, if not darkened completely, without the presence of our radiant Queen Guinevere. Her safe return, with all honor intact, shows that the Lord God in Heaven continues to bestow His favor and blessing upon the Kingdom of Logres. So let us all raise our cups and drink to the health and long life of the most noble Queen, my beloved and faithful wife, the beautiful Guinevere!

The hall now erupted in cheering and drinking. Arthur sat down again and looked over at Guinevere next to him. He thought: With such a bride by his side, the princess with the golden hair, who could doubt that he had been specially chosen by God to rule over Britain.

Later that evening, King Arthur visited his wife in her bed chamber. Once her handmaidens had left and they were alone, he again expressed his happiness at her safe return and how much more joyful Camelot was now that her presence once more graced the palace. Indeed, he noted, she remained the loveliest woman whom Arthur had ever beheld—a woman whose charms could make the moon and the stars cower in shame for their dimness and drabness.

Still, he had a question: How had Meleagant been able to kidnap her without her first raising an alarm? Why hadn't she called out for help?

Guinevere turned her eyes away from her husband before answering in a halting tone: Your Majesty recalls to mind a night that weighs heavily on my heart. Ashamed as I am to say so, I cannot remember how I came to be in the power of that criminal Meleagant. I was sleeping, as always, in this bed, under these sheets, and then the next thing I can remember I was bound on a horse charging fast through the forest toward Gorre. It is as if my memory had been enchanted—perhaps it was this enchantment that had also silenced my tongue when he first seized hold of me.

When we arrived at Meleagant's palace in Gorre, my bonds were removed, and I was escorted to a sumptuous bed chamber. The ladies of the castle washed me, scented my hair with oils, and dressed me in a white silken shift. Then they exited and Meleagant entered. He looked me over and placed his sweaty hands on my thighs and neck and hair. He tried to kiss me, but I evaded his lips.

He told me that he was my true bridegroom.

I responded that Your Majesty was my lawfully wedded husband and that I had never been pledged to any other. I told the kidnapper that Your Majesty, as a good Christian, had taken no liberties with my body until the Bishop had wed us according to the rites of the Holy Church. If Meleagant was a lawful husband, I said, and not a criminal who forces himself upon women to take what is not freely given, he would accord me the same honor.

All praise be to God and His Holy Virgin Mother, my words swayed his black heart. He swore he was no ravisher, but an honorable knight who only sought to live with his rightful bride. And so he agreed to honor my request. He told me that once he had defeated Your Majesty or your champion in a fair trial by combat, and thus had shown that God vindicated his claim to me, then he would have the priest annul my previous marriage and wed us according to the laws of the Church.

And Meleagant kept his oath—I was not touched in any shameful manner but was given fine food and clothes and treated with courtesy. Yet my heart was full of sadness, as I knew that Your Majesty was my true husband, and I could never be happy away from your love.

When Sir Lancelot arrived, my soul dared again to hope for deliverance. While I had wished that Your Majesty would have come yourself to vindicate my honor and win my freedom, I reflected that, much as this was no doubt your burning desire, your barons and your people must have begged and pleaded with you to send a champion instead, as they would no doubt be frightened of putting their sovereign's life in jeopardy. While I am sure Your Majesty fully trusted that God would have granted you a swift victory over Meleagant, as your cause was just, Your Majesty must still govern men with less steadfast faith and sometimes such lesser men, with their fears and worries, must be appeased.

After Lancelot defeated Meleagant—and may God's righteous justice fall so swiftly upon the heads of all the wicked men of this world—we left quickly. King Bagdemagus of Gorre kept his word and ensured our passage home was safe and untroubled. There could be no greater proof of the might and goodness of God than that I was delivered from such peril without being assaulted, forced, or shamed in any manner.

And now I sleep once more in Camelot, in the palace of my lord and wedded husband.

Guinevere raised her head and smiled warmly.

King Arthur smiled back at her. He heaped even more praises upon God and praised Guinevere as a model of piety and virtue and an example to all women in Christendom.

After he had finished speaking, Guinevere looked at him in a way that made Arthur think that she was freely offering her favors, should he so desire. And he should want this, he thought—he was reunited with her now, and Guinevere was so lovely in the candlelight, with her loose golden hair falling in thick waves over the red silk of her nightgown.

But there was no fire in his loins, only cold, dusty ashes. She suddenly reminded him of the statue of the Virgin Mother in the Church of St. Stephen—had he asked the sculptor to use the Queen as a model? He could not recall. But the resemblance was uncanny, and only reinforced the notion in his mind that Guinevere's beauty was of the sort to be revered and not grabbed and sweated upon.

So King Arthur gave one final thanks again to glorious God, all praise to Him and His Wonders, said that the Queen must certainly be exhausted from such a trying ordeal, and wished her a peaceful rest.

And then he left her bed chamber.

VI. Betrayal and Shame

WITH THE QUEEN rescued and no other dangers to address, King Arthur spent the next few weeks enjoying himself. He passed most of his time hunting in the forest. After a while he grew bored of chasing boars through the trees and the bushes, and so he organized tournaments to watch his finest knights charge at each other with their lances and shields. The usual victor of these games was Lancelot, who had chosen to linger about Camelot rather than return to his estates and was now widely held to be the best of Arthur's knights.

Still, Arthur did not particularly like Lancelot. There was something heavy and wearing about him. During one tournament, Lancelot's horse slipped in a patch of mud, and as a result his lance thrust missed its mark. Lancelot immediately dismounted, ran to the spot where his horse had lost its footing, and fumed that he had been sabotaged by an act of foul treachery. He was sure that an unnatural, maybe even an enchanted, liquid had been poured over the dirt in his horse's path. He demanded justice, which, in Lancelot's angry words, meant that King Arthur should strip his opponent of all his lands and titles and chop off one or more parts of the perfidious man's body.

That opponent, Sir Mordred, son of Arthur's sister Morgause, angrily protested his innocence.

Arthur gently urged Lancelot to recant his accusations and demands. Hooves slip and dirt gets wet, such are the way of things, he said. Perhaps this was God humbling a great knight after so many victories. Have some wine and rest.

The other knights and barons seated in the stands heartily agreed: Every knight eventually falls victim to a clumsy charge or a stumbling horse or a broken shield, such mishaps are not signs of treachery. Calm down, rest, drink a goblet of mead, enjoy the warm sun and laugh merrily about how God can humble any one of us when He chooses.

But Lancelot insisted that Mordred was no match for him, that his horse was the finest in Britain, and hence the only explanation for his defeat was treachery—it was blasphemous to blame God in this matter, God Whom Lancelot had always faithfully and unerringly served and Who never—never!—betrayed His true servants.

Lancelot said that the King and his highborn courtiers were not only blaspheming Holy God, but also calling him, Lancelot, a liar. They were impugning his honor. They wished to shame him. He demanded justice—he challenged all of them to a trial by combat to defend their slanders, unless they recanted their words and admitted that Mordred had cheated and thus richly deserved, to the end of his days, abject poverty, humiliation, and the severing of his legs and his ears and his thumbs.

Arthur tried again to soothe Lancelot's anger. He spoke of how men often come to regret harsh words uttered in a passionate moment and how little we sinful and mortal creatures can know of God's ways. Arthur recalled how quickly his temper would flare when he had been a young knight, but the wisdom of age flows from a calm soul and gives one the strength to put down a sword and smile meekly and humbly through the pain and embarrassment of bad luck.

But these words only inflamed Lancelot further, and he repeated his demands to joust against every nobleman in Camelot.

Yet then something unexpected happened: Queen Guinevere rose from the stands, walked down to Lancelot, and stared at him sternly, as if he were a naughty child who had stolen sweets from the kitchen. Lancelot abruptly stopped his raving and shouting, looked to the ground, mumbled a retraction of all his accusations and challenges, and slinked away.

Queen Guinevere then went back up to the stands above the tournament field and sat down again next to her husband.

King Arthur marveled at her: such was the force of her grace and her goodness that no man, no matter how demented by rage, could look her in the eye and continue to spew baseless slanders and mad threats. He silently thanked God for blessing him with such an extraordinary wife, who spread peace and courtliness wherever she turned her lovely eyes.

But then Arthur's happiness was disturbed one night, just over two weeks after Lancelot's accusations of treachery against Mordred. He was alone in his bed chamber, leaning against a tall casement window and resting his eyes on the stars hanging in the firmament. The city below was silent, and the King felt at peace with the world over which he ruled.

A guard burst in upon him. Forgive me, Your Majesty, the man began, but Sir Mordred demands an immediate audience—he is at the door—he says the matter is of the gravest importance and cannot wait until the morning.

Alarmed, Arthur ordered Mordred to be admitted at once.

Once the two men were alone, Mordred spoke: Your Majesty, I come to you reluctantly and with a heavy heart. I wish I could hold my tongue, but if I were to conceal the truth from you, as others have done, I would be as much a traitor to the throne of

Logres as they are. What I say now, I say only out of love and devotion to my lord and sovereign and to carry out the sacred oath of fealty I swore to you as your vassal.

Your Majesty no doubt recalls the day that Lancelot's horse slipped in the mud, and he slandered me with baseless accusations of treachery. I, of course, knew that God, and the honest and decent lords of Logres, would acquit me of such vile and false charges. But I was surprised that it was not the wise words of Your Majesty that swayed Lancelot from his wicked course. No, it was the displeasure of the Queen—her silent rebuke, and nothing else, made him realize the shamefulness of his conduct. He was like a vicious dog that suddenly becomes tame and meek in the presence of its one true master.

I wondered to myself how the Queen, and the Queen alone, could have such sway over Sir Lancelot's heart.

Later that same day, at the evening feast, I watched Guinevere and Lancelot. While they did not speak to one another, they exchanged many furtive glances across Your Majesty's hall, as if they had a secret understanding of some sort.

The next morning Your Majesty left the palace to hunt in the forest. As is customary and right, your lords rushed out eagerly to join you and your huntsmen. Except one: I did not see Sir Lancelot. So I decided to tell Sir Kay that I was feeling unwell and stayed back. After you had departed, I walked over to the tower where Lancelot lodges and I waited.

Soon enough, Lancelot emerged. He was dressed in a sumptuous mantle and his hair appeared freshly oiled. He moved with quick steps—impatient steps—toward the palace.

I followed him inside.

He went past the hall, up the stairs, and toward the Queen's apartments. Although I kept a discreet distance, I still clearly saw Her Majesty's handmaidens blush as Lancelot approached and, without any surprise or protest, they gave him admittance to the Lady Guinevere's private bed chamber.

Lancelot emerged again about half an hour later, his hair disheveled and a satisfied grin on his face. He walked slowly now, like a man departing from a rich banquet with a full belly, and he hummed merrily to himself.

My suspicions aroused, I followed his movements for the next three days. Each morning was the same: Once Your Majesty had left for the hunt, Lancelot rushed over to Queen Guinevere's apartments, from which he would emerge a serenely satisfied man.

At this point, I should have come to Your Majesty and revealed the betrayal of your wife and your vassal. But I hesitated. It is a grave matter to accuse the Queen of being unfaithful to her lord and husband. I had to be certain before I could burden Your Majesty's heart with the weight of such a charge.

So I had my squires drug the wine of one of Guinevere's maidservants and bring the girl to a small hunting lodge I keep a couple of hours' ride from the gates of Camelot. I had her securely bound and directed that cold water be thrown upon her face to wake her from her stupor.

Once she was alert again, I told her that several lords had discovered her lady the Queen's treachery with Lancelot and knew that she, this servant girl, had been an eager accomplice, deserving of death for having betrayed her King. However, I said that it was within my power to grant her mercy and spare her life. If she would confess her crimes freely, concealing nothing, then I would order my squires to smuggle her out of Logres on a ship bound for Ireland, where she could begin a new life.

The girl burst into tears and told me everything. She said that Lancelot and Guinevere were lovers and had lain in each other's arms many times since their return from Gorre.

I thanked her for her honesty, commended her to God, and dispatched her to Ireland in the care of my most trusted men. As soon as I returned to Camelot, I came immediately to see Your Majesty—I have brooked no delay in telling you this terrible news that your ears must hear.

Lancelot and Guinevere are traitors and adulterers. They must be arrested, at once, paraded in their shame before the people, and burned at the stake.

Arthur thanked Mordred for his loyalty and devotion, but said that he had to ponder these matters carefully and pray for guidance. In the meantime, he swore Mordred to silence.

The King passed a sleepless night. He found it hard to dispute Mordred's charges. He too had seen Guinevere and Lancelot exchange knowing looks across rooms. And he had not shared his bed with the Queen in many years. Perhaps most telling, she alone had been able to tame the rage and secure the obedience of Lancelot, who obviously feared losing her favor more than that of his lord and sovereign.

And while he did not feel jealous—after all, he had no desire to touch Guinevere himself or to while away much of his time in her company—he was nevertheless irritated with the Queen. She should have been more grateful to him. She was the daughter of a petty baron with a small castle whom Merlin had chosen to elevate to be the Queen of a great kingdom. And while she was lovely, she was barren—God was clearly unhappy with her and must have closed up her womb in punishment for some hidden but terrible sin. Many other kings—no, all other kings—would have dispatched such a barren queen to a convent and married a new, younger bride to produce an heir. But *he* had spared her that shame and humiliation. She should have had enough gratitude for his kindness to control her lusts and avoid causing him any dishonor.

And what of Logres? Her rash conduct—more fitting for a silly young maiden than a long-reigning queen—threatened to undermine his rule. No man would respect and obey a king whose wife had made him into a pathetic fool. They would laugh at him in the taverns and make up songs about how the stupid oafish husband had been so easily duped by his whoring wife's clever lies.

The only way to restore his honor would be a public show of decisive force that would prove that he was still a sovereign to be feared. He could not quietly dispatch Guinevere to a convent to live out her days in pretend piety while she had more secret trysts with her lover. No, he needed to kill her—and kill her in a manner sufficiently horrible to inspire sober, trembling awe of the mighty King Arthur's dread wrath. She needed to be tortured first, bloodied and broken and made ugly. Then have her wretched, half dead body dragged through the public square and burned to ashes. Arthur would have to stand there sternly, pitilessly, watching her flesh slowly roast and ignoring her screams of agony and pleas for mercy. Any hesitation or tears from him and the whole thing would be for naught—he would once again be the ridiculous, contemptible cuckold.

And Lancelot was just as much a traitor as she was, so he too would have to be arrested, tortured, and burned—if Arthur could capture him, as Lancelot was a fearsome knight and might escape. Still, whether Lancelot should live or die, he would be proscribed as a traitor, and his lands would be forfeited to the crown.

Although, this might force Lancelot's kinsmen to raise their arms in rebellion against Arthur.

Could all this torturing and killing be avoided? As yet the affair was still secret. Arthur could not speak to Lancelot—the man was half-mad, at least, and more likely to issue a challenge to battle than to listen to reason. Speaking to Guinevere would only be a deeper humiliation—what kind of a husband and lord pleads with his wife like a blubbering little boy to stop shaming him and to obey her sacred vows?

But then again, Arthur's thoughts continued, how long would this state of affairs continue? Women are fickle. Guinevere will tire of her lover. And Lancelot will feel the pull of duty to his kin and want a lawful wife to bear him legitimate children to inherit his titles and estates. Yes, all of this will end, probably soon. Let God judge and punish them in the next world and let Logres remain in ignorant and naive peace and happiness.

The next evening Arthur summoned Mordred back to his bed chamber for a private audience. He noticed how Mordred twitched with eagerness and excitement. Arthur wondered to himself how loyal a vassal Mordred truly was, as he seemed not to care for the difficulty of his King's position or to feel any sorrow over the Queen's betrayal.

Still, Mordred needed to be dealt with, and so Arthur spoke to him: Sir Mordred, your accusations weigh heavily on my heart, and I have considered them carefully. It is a grave and terrible matter to accuse the Queen and one of the great lords of Logres of such an awful betrayal of their sacred oaths to me. If the accusation should prove true, only the most pitiless justice could follow.

But I do not believe the accusation to be true. I have learned that the Queen has requested Lancelot to visit her from time to time to confirm that appropriate precautions are being taken to safeguard her person. I can hardly fault the Queen for her concern—she was abducted from her bed in this very palace by that wretch Meleagant. Thus, it appears to me that the meetings between them are wholly innocent. It is your base envy and lewd imagination which have conjured up such revolting scenes of vile carnal lust. You should reflect long and hard upon the state of your soul and why you have been so quick, so eager even, to assume there is such dreadful sin afoot. Perhaps it is you who is tormented by temptation? Perhaps you should speak to your confessor and consider a period of penitence and fasting to cleanse yourself?

As to the servant girl whom you questioned, she is lowborn, and she was brought here as an act of Christian charity by the Queen. You cannot truly believe that the testimony of such a person is sufficient to impeach the conduct of those born from noble blood.

And even if she is an honest maiden—and I find it quite doubtful that the bastard child of some peasant whore would be an honest maiden—you kidnapped, bound, and threatened her. She would have said anything you wanted to hear to get herself released to safety.

You have been overzealous in this matter and fallen into error and confusion. In order to provide an opportunity for you to reflect upon your intemperate actions, I shall send you as my envoy to Rome to deliver certain sacred relics to His Holiness the Pope, so that pilgrims from across all of Christendom may seek their aid—our island of Britain being too cold and too distant for so many good Christians. There will be many abbeys and hermitages along the way where you can be confessed, hear Mass, and pray for guidance from Our Lord and Savior and His Holy Virgin Mother.

Finally, remember well the oath of silence you swore to me. Speak of this matter again, to anyone, and *you* will be forsworn and proscribed as a traitor to the Kingdom of Logres.

Now you may take your leave. It has been a difficult day, and I must rest.

Mordred looked at Arthur, his eyes pulsating with hate and anger, but he held his tongue and said nothing. After a moment's hesitation, Mordred bowed and left.

VII. The Queen's Tale

AS QUEEN GUINEVERE was riding on the back of Meleagant's swift horse, a prisoner bound tightly with rough ropes on her way to a castle in faraway Gorre, she reflected that she did not know herself very well. Guinevere had always been careful to conduct herself as a praiseworthy and courteous Queen, a faithful Christian, and an honest and true wife. While it was true that her husband and lord, King Arthur, had often disappointed her in his coldness, she had never let his conduct be an excuse for acting dishonorably and demeaning herself. When Meleagant had entered her bed chamber in the middle of the night, a grimly determined silhouette in the yellow moonlight, bounding toward her, sword at his side, what she ought to have done as a faithful wife was quite clear: resist to the utmost and cry out for help as loudly as she could.

But she did not resist. And she did not cry out. Instead, when he leaned over her, the ropes in his hands, she calmly sat up and extended herself meekly and silently into his power. She then followed obediently as he led her away—she even took care to muffle the sound of her steps by walking on the carpets and avoiding the stone floor.

It was not until the sun was rising the next day, and Meleagant was well on his way with her to Gorre, that it occurred to Guinevere that she had acted shamefully—that anyone who knew how willingly she had let herself be taken captive would be convinced that she had intended to betray her husband.

So why had she let herself be kidnapped? She was not sure. There was something shameful, if not evil, in her soul, she thought. There must be—nothing else could explain why she had acquiesced in her own abduction.

As it turned out, Meleagant was more honorable than she had expected him to be. When they arrived at his castle, he escorted her to a sumptuous bedroom, explained that her every need would be seen to by her new maidservants, and swore that he would scrupulously respect the sanctity of her person until he had proven in combat that she was his rightful bride and they had been wed according to proper Church rites. Good to his word, he then left without even trying to steal a kiss or touch her hand.

At that moment, Guinevere felt a tinge of disappointment, even though she told herself she should be grateful that God had protected her from disgrace. She tried to offer up a prayer of thanksgiving that her kidnapper was not demanding to lie with her in his bed—but the words refused to form in her throat. Instead, she attempted to sleep, but a tingling and twitching in her limbs kept her from properly resting.

She remained in this agitated and confused state until Lancelot arrived at Meleagant's stronghold in Gorre. She was disappointed that her husband had not come, but she reminded herself that King Arthur was too important to be risked in a single combat—upon the thin thread of his life alone hung the peace and prosperity of Logres.

Guinevere watched Lancelot in the meadow below the castle gates as he readied himself for battle. She marveled at his figure, so tall, strong, and graceful on his horse. He handled his heavy, iron-tipped lance as if it weighed nothing at all. Guinevere felt better: Her husband did truly love her, with real passionate devotion, because otherwise he would not have sent such a handsome, virile champion to vindicate her honor.

After Meleagant's defeat and death, she and Lancelot set out together on the road back to Logres, a journey of several days. The first night, in a small clearing by the forest road, Lancelot pitched a tent for the Queen. As she was lying down on a blanket spread over the grass, Lancelot fell down at her feet and declared that she was the most beautiful and worthy woman in all the Christian and heathen kingdoms of the world, that he had yearned for so long for her affection—yearned so desperately for the favor of merely a brief, flickering smile thrown his way—and that he swore now, upon all that has ever been holy and true, that he would devote his life to her service, to obey her in every wish. Nothing was too trivial.

In response, Guinevere braced herself. She was sure he would now demand to lie with her right then and there—to enjoy the favors of her body as recompense for having freed from her captivity. In her mind, she pictured him removing his armor and looming over her, naked, muscular, breathing hard and fast in his passion.

But instead, he remained trembling at her feet, chastely and honorably, awaiting her command.

Realizing that Lancelot would not move until she said something, Guinevere thanked him for his kind words, offered him the favor of her smile, and bade him guard her person well that night from wolves and robbers.

Blushing all over, Lancelot stammered out his humble gratitude for the favor of her smile and swore he would lay down his life before he would let any harm befall the most extraordinary, marvelous, and perfect specimen of womanhood ever fashioned by the blessed Creator of the land and the sky. With that, Lancelot left her alone in the tent to rest.

The next morning, Guinevere decided to test whether Lancelot truly intended to render her every service she might request of him. Hence, she asked him to go to a nearby tree, pick an apple, and peel away the skin in one continuous coil—if the skin should be broken off in more than one continuous spiraling piece, he would need to start over with a new apple. Lancelot immediately obeyed without complaint, even though he ultimately had to pick and peel more than a dozen apples before he could present to Her Majesty an apple that had been peeled in the exact manner she had demanded.

Feeling amused, she then had him do all sorts of other odd and degrading tasks: She had him take her shoes off and on several times, fetch water from dangerous rapids only to spill it on the ground, and wash all her garments in a stream. Each time, Lancelot eagerly obeyed and thanked her for the honor of being her meekest servant and most ardent admirer.

At first, Guinevere felt slightly guilty about humiliating the knight who had rescued her, but soon she noticed that every time she asked Lancelot to do another task, his face lit up with a radiant glow. When she was not ordering him about, he looked at her silently, but intently, poised to jump at her least word. His mind seemed to have room for nothing but her.

That night, she summoned Lancelot inside her tent.

He immediately obeyed.

She ordered him to undress for her, completely, as she lay in her shift on top of a blanket.

Once more, he obeyed.

And then Guinevere waited. She was certain he would approach her now and try to act on his love. She was not entirely sure if she wanted him to or not. While she felt a great desire for Lancelot, she also felt shame—she was a Christian woman who had sworn a holy oath to her husband, and she was on the verge of breaking it. But then again, his nude body, muscular and trembling in the twilight shining through the tent's thin walls, was a sight to behold.

Yet Lancelot did nothing. He stood there above her in his beautiful nakedness, his eyes turned bashfully upon the ground.

The silence between them lasted for a long time. However, the mounting tension only heightened Guinevere's desire and at last she summoned him to her side. And then they did what lovers do.

Their affair continued for the rest of the journey back to Logres. Traveling through the dense forests, with only Lancelot to keep her company, Guinevere felt as if she had entered a magical realm where everything she had thought was real—husband, royal court, church—ceased to exist, and she could indulge her most passionate and whimsical fancies without any shame or guilt.

By the time she returned to Camelot, she was bursting with happiness. But she was also glad to be leaving behind the pleasures of the journey through the forest. It felt good to return to the comforts of her husband's palace and she looked forward to resuming her duties as Queen of Logres.

Guinevere assumed that, after a couple of days of feasting and humbly receiving new estates from King Arthur in honor of his triumph, Lancelot would return to his own castle and lands. He would need a wife. She had to give some thought to which noble lady at court would suit him best—the woman had to be beautiful and highborn and full of Christian faith—and also strong enough not to be crushed beneath the passion of such an ardent lover. Guinevere felt giddy at the thought of finding a bride for Lancelot: a suitable service for her to perform in recompense and gratitude for the many services, and pleasures, he had rendered to her.

But to her surprise, Lancelot lingered at Camelot. He followed her around the hallways of the palace and stared wide-eyed at her when she gave alms to the poor or received noble ladies at court. He always seemed to be looking for an opportunity to accost her somewhere or somehow. She worried that his conduct would draw unwelcome attention and raise uncomfortable questions. He seemed not to grasp the difference between traveling together in an isolated forest road, where there was no shame, and life in a capital city teeming with people to whom she owed many obligations, including her lawfully wedded husband, the King of Logres.

She tried to avoid him—turning corners sharply when she saw him approaching, gliding to the other side of rooms to keep her distance, rushing into church pews surrounded by a protective phalanx of genuflecting handmaidens. But despite her careful and judicious conduct, the import of which she was sure that he must have understood, Lancelot kept following her wherever she went, gazing after her with a look of baffled longing and pain.

The Queen eventually concluded that she had to speak to him about his conduct. She sent a servant to Lancelot to ask him to visit her rooms shortly after Arthur and his knights were to leave in the morning for the hunt. The servant reported back that Lancelot had fallen to the ground in front of her, kissed her feet, and thanked her for giving him the message that had made him again the happiest man in Christendom.

Hearing these words, Guinevere felt a sudden sense of dread.

The next morning Lancelot appeared promptly in answer to her summons. His beauty was in full bloom: His perfumed blond hair was long and thick about his shoulders, and his burgundy mantle tightly hugged his broad chest and muscular arms. She gasped involuntarily—his lovely form had a way of going to her head too fast, like a strong brandy.

After Guinevere dismissed her attendants and they were alone, Lancelot fell to his knees. His love for her, he declared, had not wavered in the slightest, even though she had cruelly shunned

him. He knew she could not be so pitiless as to leave him in this
wretched state unless he had wronged her in some way. He begged
her forgiveness for every word or act that had failed to show
enough devotion to the most beautiful and wise and good of
women, the greatest lady to walk the Earth since the days of the
one and only woman blessed to give birth as a virgin to the Savior
Himself.

He hoped she would accept the penance he had undergone by
writhing in agony in the absence of her smiles and kisses and
caresses. Would she have the merciful heart to take him again into
her arms?

Guinevere was uneasy. Although she still desired Lancelot,
she was revolted at the thought of lying with him in the bed where
her lawfully wedded husband had once embraced her. But would
he leave Camelot if she told him to? Or would he do something so
mad and desperate that it would expose their past adultery to
Arthur and the rest of the court?

No, her thoughts continued, better not to goad him into even
more grandiose proofs of his love. He needed to be cured of her,
that was clear. She needed to set him a task so repugnant to his
honor that he would abandon her of his own volition rather than
comply.

Guinevere addressed him, weighing her words carefully:

My dear Lancelot, you are right. You have wronged me. I will
not review each of your foul deeds and petty betrayals. You know
them well enough, and I trust that during your penance you have
often reflected upon them.

You still claim to be a faithful lover, trumpeting all these
exalted praises for the lady whom you would serve. But words are
easy to scatter about. When we ladies of the court are bored, we
toss coins at minstrels to serve up heaping platters of flattery for
our beauty and our virtues. Give the minstrel a few more coins,

and out he spews a few more praises for my beauty and my virtue. A coin, a word; thus is the value of men's words.

But deeds, bold deeds that prove the truth and constancy of a man's love, those are another matter. Minstrels may sing of knightly deeds; but ask one of them to mount a horse and level a lance and he will run away like a terrified rabbit, no matter how many coins I throw at his head.

Only your deeds can prove that you are genuinely contrite and worthy once again of receiving my favors. Do you swear, upon all that is holy and dear to you in this world and the next, that you will perform whatever service I demand of you?

I swear! I swear! Please, my lady, my love, tell me your wish and I will gladly do it this very instant. No task is too daunting to win back your affection.

Are you willing to do as I ask, even if it shall bring you only shame and ridicule?

I will joyfully embrace the mockery of others if that is the price to be your beloved.

Then I suppose I shall see if your deeds will match your words. As you have sworn to undergo the test, I will set you to prove your love. Here it is: In two days' time, my husband, His Majesty King Arthur, is holding a tournament on the meadow just beyond the walls of Camelot. You will enter the lists. You will joust against Sir Mordred, son of King Arthur's sister, the noble Lady Morgause. You will let Mordred unhorse you and defeat you. You will loudly and clearly acknowledge Mordred as the victor and the superior knight, in front of King Arthur and all his knights and barons. That is the penance I demand of you.

Guinevere was sure that Lancelot would now refuse and leave in a fit of rage. To be defeated by a renowned knight like Gawain or Sagremor would be no shame, but no one respected Mordred. To fall to Mordred's pitifully inept lance would be a bitter humiliation.

Guinevere's hopes swelled as she watched Lancelot look down, turn red, and seemingly strain to check his anger. Yet after a couple of minutes of silence, Lancelot raised his head again, looked her in the eye and said, carefully articulating each word, that he would always obey the command of his beloved.

And then he took his leave.

On the day of the tournament, Guinevere sat next to Arthur in the stands. She saw Lancelot ride forth and announce his name to the crier to be added to the lists. Then he issued a challenge to Sir Mordred.

Guinevere noticed that Arthur shot him an angry and disapproving look—her husband no doubt thought, she mused, that Lancelot should choose a worthier opponent. But Lancelot ignored his lord and sovereign.

As the knights drew away from each other to prepare to charge, Guinevere was hopeful once again. Lancelot was a powerful and skilled knight; his instincts would surely overtake his reason and without thinking he would quickly knock Mordred to the ground, giving her an excuse to reject his love and banish him from Camelot.

But in the next instant it was Lancelot who was thrown to the ground, rolling in the dirt, and Mordred was loudly proclaiming his unexpected victory. Although at first seemingly stunned speechless, Arthur and his knights and his barons soon roared with applause for the winner of the joust, for whom they clearly appeared to have a newfound respect.

Meanwhile, Guinevere watched Lancelot. He had removed his helmet, and there was a gash on his forehead dripping blood into his eyes. He was watching Mordred boast and celebrate, and his expression narrowed into a dark grimace.

Then Lancelot rose back to his feet and approached Mordred.

Everyone now fell silent.

Lancelot pointed his finger at Mordred and, in a voice quivering with rage, accused Mordred of vile and base treachery, of using underhanded tricks to seize an unfair victory over a superior knight.

Guinevere watched her husband and his counselors try to calm Lancelot's wrath and persuade him to recant his harsh words. But this only led Lancelot to accuse even more men of treachery, and he started issuing challenges to battle to every nobleman there.

Guinevere realized she had to put a stop to this wild behavior before Lancelot murdered someone. She walked down from the stands to the jousting grounds and approached him. At the sight of her and her reproving eyes, Lancelot suddenly fell silent and walked sheepishly away from the meadow.

The next morning, after Arthur had once again departed to hunt game in the forest, Lancelot demanded to be admitted to the Queen's bed chamber.

Guinevere granted him permission to enter.

Just as before, he fell to his knees. My lady, my love, object of my every desire and devotion, he began, I have done the task you had set for me and willingly degraded myself before all the knights of Logres—I have made a mockery of myself. Is this not penance enough for my sins against your love? Will you not take pity upon my suffering? I cannot sleep or eat, for all I can think of is how much I long for you. You *must* take pity on my suffering, I beg you, and grant me your favors once again. My reason cannot hold out much longer.

Guinevere looked into his eyes, bloodshot and puffy from sleepless nights, and, for the first time, she was afraid. What if his reason truly did fall to pieces? What would he do? He could start challenging and killing knights and barons, as he had threatened to do after Mordred had unhorsed him. Or perhaps he would make a public proclamation of their love—even reveal what they had done together in the forests of Gorre—she would be shamed forevermore, divorced, and cast out as an adulterous whore.

No, she told herself, she would not let such calamities come to pass. She would appease Lancelot. Let the fire in his blood be extinguished by having his passion satisfied. Guinevere reasoned that once men satisfy the cravings of their flesh, their love fades fast, and they wander off to hunt or sleep or, even better, they start yearning for a new mistress.

She bade him rise and undress. She withdrew to the bed, lay down on her back, and waited. But this time, when he seized her in his strong arms, she felt no passion, only worries—would they be discovered? Could they be overheard? Would her handmaidens keep her secret?

She wished it would end quickly. She felt sharp pains as his sweaty body thrashed about inside of her. She tried to use her eyes to urge Lancelot to hurry up and be finished, but his gaze seemed to be lost in another world, where he was savoring the delights of some imagined Paradise.

Eventually he finished, which came as a relief to Guinevere—the same relief, she thought, as when a snake's venom is sucked from a wound. Lancelot lazily dressed himself again, kissed her hand, pledged his eternal and undying devotion, and left before she could speak in response.

Guinevere collapsed back onto her bed and slept for a long time. She hoped that his love would now fade. After all, he had nothing further to gain from it.

Yet the next morning, he returned to her rooms, once more falling at her feet and begging for her favors. And out of fear of what he might do, or say, if she refused, she reluctantly yielded her flesh to his entreaties and braced for the awful, dry pain that her loins would be forced to endure.

And then Lancelot came a third day. But this time he scolded her: My lady, he said, you are too cruel to your lover. You offer up the favors of your body, but with a coldness of spirit, like a miser who only gives alms with great reluctance. Why do you treat me with such malice and spite? Have I not suffered enough for your love?

Guinevere felt a chill in her blood at the idea of being forced to pretend to be in the throes of a passion she did not feel. But then she thought of a ruse to gain some relief from Lancelot's unwelcome attentions:

My dear Lancelot, can a lady offer a love that is complete in exchange for a love that is not equally pure? You would have me trade a gold cup inlaid with rubies for a clay vessel painted with little red dots. You wish for an exalted love, but have you shown yourself worthy? Yes, you obeyed my command to fall to defeat before Mordred, but then you accused Mordred of treachery and cheating. You did *not* willingly endure the ordeal of humiliation I demanded as your penance, and you left a lingering doubt in other men's minds that Mordred's victory was not genuine. Thus, you both obeyed and defied my command to you. In turn, I both give myself and deny myself to you.

If you wish for a love complete, then you must prove yourself worthy. You must ride into the Broceliande Forest and achieve three marvelous adventures that will astound the court at Camelot. And from each adventure, you must bring me back a special token of your love.

Without any hesitation, Lancelot swore to ride off immediately to find and conquer the adventures his beloved demanded. He swore that he would prove himself to be worthy of her love—her true and complete love.

The next day, King Arthur and Queen Guinevere together bid farewell and good fortune to Sir Lancelot on his quest for new adventures and to Sir Mordred on his embassy to His Holiness the Pope in Rome. Guinevere noted that Arthur seemed unusually happy to see them both go from Camelot, and he did his best to hurry along the leave-taking.

With Lancelot gone at last, Guinevere felt suddenly exhausted and retired early to her bed. Her dreams were easy and joyful—of bright unclouded days and fragrant flowers, of pretty sunsets over the seashore and gently crashing waves on the beach.

When she woke the next morning, the sun was just starting to rise. She dressed quickly, left the palace, and went to the still empty Church of St. Stephen. There, she knelt down before the statue of the Holy Virgin Mother and prayed.

Queen Guinevere prayed for many things: for the peace and prosperity of Logres; for the remaining heathens of Britain to embrace the one true faith of Christianity and to accept baptism; and for the wisdom to guide the young maidens who had come to the court at Camelot into felicitous marriages with fine husbands of noble character and unyielding faith in God.

But despite her best efforts, her soul refused to stay focused on these honorable prayers. Instead, as her eyes looked up at the statue of the Virgin Mary, she pictured Lancelot, in all his naked, taut beauty, kissing and caressing the marble statue, writhing upon it with his muscular limbs. And at his touch, the marble grew hot, and the pale cheeks of the holy saint blushed and glowed like burning coals. Guinevere felt her flesh tingle and vibrate, ever so subtly, and a sweet warmth rushed through her veins. And now, once more, she felt free to dream her wonderful dreams of love.

Other Books by Barak Bassman

Elegy of the Minotaur

Repentance: A Tale of Demons in Old Jewish Poland

King Solomon and Ashmedai: A Wisdom Tale

The Twilight of the Magical Siren: A Tale of Late Antiquity

The Leper Princess and The Court Jew

The Last Confession of Joseph della Reina

The Gifts of the Fairy Melusine

*Necromancy of the Demon Maiden:
A Gothic Tale of Podolia*

The Death of the Wizard Merlin

The Vampire and The Wandering Jew

The Emissary from Mezeritch: A Dark Hasidic Tale

The Beheading Game: An Arthurian Tale

The Holy Sinner: A Gothic Tale of the Baal Shem Tov